can bi 4

Note to parents and carers

Read it yourself is a series of modern stories, favourite characters and traditional tales written in a simple way for children who are learning to read. The books can be read independently or as part of a guided reading session.

Each book is carefully structured to include many high-frequency words vital for first reading. The sentences on each page are supported closely by pictures to help with understanding, and to offer lively details to talk about.

The books are graded into four levels that progressively introduce wider vocabulary and longer stories as a reader's ability and confidence grows.

Ideas for use

- Begin by looking through the book and talking about the pictures. Has your child heard this story before?

- Help your child with any words he does not know, either by helping him to sound them out or supplying them yourself.

- Developing readers can be concentrating so hard on the words that they sometimes don't fully grasp the meaning of what they're reading. Answering the puzzle questions on pages 30 and 31 will help with understanding.

For more information and advice on Read it yourself and book banding, visit **www.ladybird.com/readityourself**

Book
Band
4

Level 1 is ideal for children who have received some initial reading instruction. Each story is told very simply, using a small number of frequently repeated words.

Special features:

Opening pages introduce key story words

bird

Rose the fairy

Lily the fairy

cat

Patch the elf

Large, clear type

Rose saw a dog. "We can help that dog," she said.
Lily and Rose went to help the dog.

Careful match between story and pictures

Educational Consultant: Geraldine Taylor
Book Banding Consultant: Kate Ruttle

A catalogue record for this book is available from the British Library

Published by Ladybird Books Ltd
80 Strand, London, WC2R 0RL
A Penguin Company

002

ISBN: 978-0-71819-465-9

Printed in China

Fairy Friends

Written by Ronne Randall
Illustrated by Joelle Driedemy

Rose
the fairy

Lily
the fairy

bird

cat

Patch
the elf

Lily was a fairy and Rose was a fairy, too.

Lily and Rose liked to help their friends.

Lily saw a bird. "We can help that bird," she said.

Lily and Rose helped the bird.

Rose saw a cat. "Now we can help that cat," she said.

Lily and Rose helped the cat.

Lily saw a mouse.

"Now we can help that mouse," she said.

It was not a mouse! It was Patch, a bad elf. Patch liked to play tricks.

He had turned into a mouse to trick Lily and Rose.

Rose saw a dog. "We can help that dog," she said.

Lily and Rose went to help the dog.

It was not a dog. It was Patch the elf! He had turned into a dog to trick Lily and Rose.

"Go away, Patch!" said Lily and Rose. "You are a bad elf!"

Lily saw a fairy. "We can help that fairy," she said.

"That is not a fairy," said Rose. "It is Patch. Go away, Patch, you bad elf!"

They saw the fairy, and they saw Patch, too!

"It IS a fairy," said Rose.

"We can help you," said Lily.

Lily and Rose
helped the fairy.

Patch turned into a bird
and he helped, too.

The fairy was Lily and Rose's new friend.

Now Patch was their friend, too.

How much do you remember about the story of Fairy Friends? Answer these questions and find out!

- **What do Lily and Rose like to do?**

- **Who tricks Lily and Rose?**

- **Can you remember two of the animals Patch turned into?**

Look at the pictures from the story and say the order they should go in.

A

B

C

D

Answer: C, D, B, A.

Read it yourself with Ladybird

Tick the books you've read!

For children who are ready to take their first steps in reading.

Level 1

The Enormous Turnip

Fairy Friends

Goldilocks and the Three Bears

Little Red Hen

The Magic Porridge Pot

Little Creatures

Recycling Fun!

The Princess and the Pea

Cinderella

Rex the Big Dinosaur

The Tale of Peter Rabbit

The Three Billy Goats Gruff

Why Giraffe has a Long Neck

Go to the Zoo

The Ugly Duckling

The Emperor's New Clothes

For beginner readers who can read short, simple sentences with help.

Level 2

Beauty and the Beast

Chicken Licken

Little Red Riding Hood

Nature Trail

Sports Day

Pirate School

Rumpelstiltskin

Sleeping Beauty

The Gingerbread Man

Sly Fox and Red Hen

The Tale of Jemima Puddle-Duck

The Three Little Pigs

Why Lion Roarrrs!

The Big Race

Town Mouse and the Country Mouse

Dom's Dragon

The Read it yourself with Ladybird app is now available for iPad, iPhone and iPod touch

App also available on Android devices